The Dog

John Burningham

CANDLEWICK PRESS
CAMBRIDGE, MASSACHUSETTS

One day a dog
we know was
left at our house
for a visit.

Mommy said
I could take
care of him.

He ate the
cat's lunch.

He licked me.

He ran into
the yard with
Daddy's shoe.

And he peed
on the flowers.

Then he
dug a hole
in the yard.

So I put him
on his leash.

I wish the
dog could
stay with me.

Copyright © 1975 by John Burningham

Second U.S. edition 1994
First published in Great Britain in 1975
by Jonathan Cape Ltd., London.

Library of Congress Cataloging-in-Publication Data

Burningham, John.
The dog / John Burningham.— 2nd U.S. ed.
"First published in Great Britain in 1975
by Jonathan Cape Ltd., London"—T.p. verso.
Summary: A small boy enjoys looking after a dog
that is staying at his home awhile.
ISBN 1-56402-326-5
[1. Dogs—Fiction.] I. Title.
PZ7.B936Do   1994
[E]—dc20   93-10344

10 9 8 7 6 5 4 3 2 1

Printed in Hong Kong

The pictures in this book were done in pastels, crayon, and ink.

Candlewick Press
2067 Massachusetts Avenue
Cambridge, Massachusetts 02140